A Winter Solstice Celebration

Written by DiDi LeMay
Illustrated by Jacquie Campbell

To Sabrina,
may all your
dreams &
wishes come
true!
DiDi

AuthorHouse™
1663 Liberty Drive, Suite 200
Bloomington, IN 47403
www.authorhouse.com
Phone: 1-800-839-8640

First published by AuthorHouse September 17, 2008

ISBN: 978-1-4389-0998-1 (sc)

Library of Congress Control Number: 2008907905

Edited by Maria Jelinek
Photographer Nir Bareket

Printed in the United States of America
Bloomington, Indiana

This book is printed on acid-free Post Consumer Waste paper.

DEDICATED TO

THE CHILDREN OF THE WORLD.
LET'S JOIN TOGETHER, TO HELP OUR PLANET.

ACKNOWLEDGEMENTS

I WOULD LIKE TO ACKNOWLEDGE ALL MY FRIENDS, FAMILY AND ANYONE ELSE WHO HAS SUPPORTED ME DURING THE WRITING OF THIS BOOK. A HEART FELT THANK YOU TO ALL OF YOU. I KNOW YOU KNOW WHO YOU ARE!

DIDI

THE WINTER SOLSTICE

The Winter Solstice is a very old celebration. In ancient times, people all over the world celebrated this festival. Winter Solstice occurs the moment that the sun's position in the sky is at its greatest distance to the equator.
The Winter Solstice happens between December 20 and December 23 each year in the Northern Hemisphere. In the Southern Hemisphere, it happens between June 20 and June 23. It occurs on the day of the year with the least amount of daylight time.
Though the Winter Solstice lasts an instant, the word can also be used to describe the full 24-hour day.
People from different cultures have celebrated this festival in many different ways. The Viking, Inca, Myan, Egyptian, Asian, Islamic, and Scandinavian cultures were some of the people who celebrated the Winter Solstice.
There are still people in the world today that celebrate the winter solstice.

The Village near the forest

Hidden in the valley, close to the forest where all the animals lived, lay a small village. The red brick houses with their thatched roofs and black shutters were built in neat little rows. They lined the cobblestone streets like little soldiers at attention. Some of the houses had small stone walls built around the gardens. Others had thick, green hedges where mice and hedgehogs lived. You could imagine what the gardens looked like in the summer with their colourful flowers, buzzing bees, lively birds, and butterflies fluttering from branch to branch.

Now, in the winter, the flowers had withered and the leaves had fallen from the trees. The birds and bees were sleeping and snow covered the ground, hedges, trees, and rooftops. Little snowdrifts piled up against the windowsills. Puffs of smoke wafted from the chimneys as icicles hung from the rooftops.

The village square stood right in the middle of the village. There were benches scattered throughout the square. The cobblestones that paved the square were now covered with a light dusting of soft, white snow. A grocery store, a bakery, a butcher shop, and a post office lined the square.

It was a cold and cloudy afternoon. The villagers, bundled in warm coats and woollen hats, hurried from one store to another to buy gifts for their families and friends. They were preparing for the approaching winter solstice celebrations. Colourful decorations were displayed in the windows next to all the shiny, new gifts.

The church, built with grey stone walls and stained glass windows, stood to the left of the square, proud and tall. A few children sat on the church steps laughing and playing. They were dressed in brightly coloured winter jackets and warm fleece hats and scarves. If you stood at the top of the church steps and looked down the main road, you could see the treetops of the forest in the distance.

The village's main road led directly past fields and meadows to the forest. The forest was a beautiful and peaceful place. The villagers and their children often visited the forest on a Sunday afternoon, escaping the hustle and bustle of day to day life in the village.

In the distance, Miya, a young girl who lived in the village, skipped along the icy road that led to the forest. She was dressed in a bright blue winter jacket and wore a white woollen hat on top of her curly, brown hair. She had a cozy scarf wrapped around her neck to keep her warm. Her cheeks were rosy-red and her eyes shone brightly, because she was very excited to be going to feed the animals in the forest. Miya dug her hands deep into her big pockets to keep them warm from the blustery wind. As she walked along the lane, she clutched a small bundle under her arm.

WHILE SHE SKIPPED ALONG, SHE WHISTLED A HAPPY TUNE AND LOOKED AROUND. THE GREY, WINTRY SKY LOOKED CHEERLESS. IT SEEMED THAT THE TREES, BARE MEADOWS, AND FROZEN DITCHES WERE WAITING FOR WARMER TIMES. A COLD GUST OF WIND BLEW ACROSS THE FIELDS. MIYA SHIVERED AS SHE GOT CLOSER AND CLOSER TO THE FOREST THAT PROTECTED THE BLEAK AND FROSTY MEADOWS.

MIYA'S MOTHER HAD TAUGHT HER HOW TO RESPECT ANIMALS AND THE ENVIRONMENT. THIS MORNING, SHE HAD GIVEN MIYA A FEW OLD LOAVES OF BREAD AND SOME STALE BISCUITS TO PUT OUT FOR THE ANIMALS, SO THAT THEY WOULD NOT GO HUNGRY. HER MOTHER HAD TOLD MIYA TO LOOK AFTER THE ANIMALS AND HELP THEM IN TIMES OF NEED. SHE HAD ALSO TOLD MIYA THAT SOMETIMES IN THE WINTER FOOD WAS SCARCE FOR THE ANIMALS, AND IT WAS KIND TO HELP THEM. MIYA HAD TAKEN HER OWN LUNCH TOO, BECAUSE SHE WANTED TO SPEND SOME TIME EXPLORING THE FOREST. MAYBE SHE WOULD SEE SOME OF THE ANIMALS. SHE LOVED ANIMALS, AND SHE ALWAYS DREAMED OF MEETING THEM SOMEDAY.

ANXIOUSLY, MIYA LOOKED UP TO THE SKY AND NOTICED THAT THE CLOUDS WERE DARK. IN A THREATENING MANNER, THEY HUNG LOW OVER THE DESERTED FIELDS AND TREES. SNOW WOULD FALL ANY MINUTE. SHE QUICKLY MARCHED TOWARDS THE FOREST BEFORE IT STARTED TO SNOW.

MIYA SLOWLY ENTERED THE BIG FOREST, OVERWHELMED BY THE TALL FIR TREES. SHE FELT PROTECTED AS THE TREES CLOSED AROUND HER. THERE WAS AN ICY MIST AMONG THE TREES, AND MIYA SHIVERED. AS MIYA LOOKED UP AT THE TREETOPS, A SINGLE SNOWFLAKE FELL ON HER UPTURNED FACE. SHE GIGGLED. THAT WAS COLD!

IT WAS EERILY QUIET, BUT OCCASIONALLY A BIRD CRIED OUT TO TELL HER SHE WAS NOT ALONE. SHE QUICKLY SCATTERED BREAD AND BISCUITS ACROSS A SMALL CLEARING. EVERY TIME SHE PUT MORE FOOD OUT, SHE NOTICED THAT THE OLD BREAD WAS GONE, AND SHE KNEW THAT THE ANIMALS HAD FOUND IT. MIYA SMILED. THIS MADE HER VERY HAPPY, BECAUSE SHE KNEW THE ANIMALS WOULD NOT BE HUNGRY.

Not obeying her mother who had told her to come straight home, she wandered deeper and deeper into the forest. She was very curious about the animals. After a while, Miya could hear her belly growling. She was hungry and tired. She sat on the frozen ground. It was covered with pine needles. Miya opened the package she had brought from home, pulled out a sandwich, and ate it. When she had finished her lunch, she lay back, snuggled into her warm jacket, and stared dreamily up towards the sky.

After a few minutes, Miya felt she wasn't alone. Slowly, she turned her head and jumped up in surprise. In front of her sat a squirrel. His paws were crossed in front of his chest, and he had a frown on his furry face. The little animal glared at Miya. She stared back, a little astonished.

"What are you doing here?" asked the squirrel angrily.

"Well, I··· I···" stammered Miya, stunned. The animal was talking.

He swished his bushy tail, and he yelled furiously, "Leave our forest! Now!" With those unfriendly words, he ran off, into the bushes.

Miya watched in amazement as the squirrel ran away. She sighed. For a moment she just stood there, not sure of what to do. She had just spoken to a squirrel. Rather, he had spoken to her. This was a significant experience. The squirrel had told her to leave immediately. Miya had to decide what to do. She wanted to be friends with the animals and didn't want to make them angry. But she also wanted to explore the forest. Of course, this was their place, and if she wasn't welcome, well, she should leave quietly.

With a shrug of her shoulders, Miya decided it would be better to listen to the squirrel and go home. She picked up her belongings. Being careful she didn't leave any garbage behind, she turned to walk to the edge of the forest. Thinking about the experience with the squirrel, Miya walked and walked.

After a few minutes, Miya stopped and looked around. Nothing seemed familiar. She wasn't sure which way to go. She turned right, took a few steps, then paused and started walking in the opposite direction. Miya did not recognize where she was. With a sigh, she miserably sank onto an old tree stump and groaned. "All the trees look alike. I think I'm lost."

Miya sat there for a few moments and wondered what to do next, when she heard a commotion. Her face brightened. It seemed that there were more people from the village visiting the forest. She wasn't alone. Miya jumped up and started running towards the direction of the voices.

Miya meets the animals

Boy, how she ran! She leapt over the fallen trees, crashing through the bushes, and she fell. She scrambled up again, scraping her hands and knees. Once in a while, she stopped to listen for the voices. Ignoring her bruised hands and scraped knees, Miya continued to run until she reached a clearing in the woods. Here she stumbled upon all sorts of animals. Standing there, eye to eye, she was as surprised as they were.

THE SQUIRREL, WHOM SHE HAD MET BEFORE, STEPPED FORWARD. HE WAS MOODY AND DID NOT LIKE THE HUMANS. HIS COUSIN, WHO LIVED IN THE VILLAGE, HAD TOLD HIM STORIES ABOUT THE VILLAGERS AND THE OTHER HUMANS IN THE CITY. THEY WERE ALL BAD STORIES. IT SEEMED THAT THEY DID NOT THINK ABOUT THE CONSEQUENCES OF THEIR ACTIONS. THE GIRL WAS ONE OF THEM!

The squirrel moved forward and said angrily, "Hey! Why are you here? Didn't I tell you to leave?"

"Well, yes… yes you did," stammered Miya. "But, but… I got lost." She burst into tears.

"Oh, little girl, ne'er mind 'im," spoke a crackly, old voice.

Miya looked up and blinked. Through her tears, she saw a big black crow with shiny feathers standing right next to her. With his dark, friendly eyes, he looked her up and down. His enormous yellow beak pointed towards the squirrel. The crow seemed to be a gentle and kind old bird.

"That squirrel," the crow said. "Well, he's just a grumpy old guy."

"Humph," said the squirrel, turning his back to Miya and the crow. He stomped towards a clump of bushes, where he sat brooding.

Miya nodded, her brown curls bouncing up and down. She sniffed and wiped her tears on the sleeve of her blue coat. She pulled her white hat tightly over her head. Then she looked around curiously.

There was a cluster of old tree stumps that stood to one side, covered with a sprinkling of soft, white snow. Right beside the tree stumps was a hollow tree trunk with a layer of velvety, green moss. In one corner, near an old, gnarly oak tree, a few of the smaller animals huddled together nervously. They shifted from one foot to the other. They stuck their sensitive, little, black noses in the air to smell if the girl was a good human or a bad one.

Miya's arrival in the clearing had disturbed a meeting. The owl was the chairperson, and she was very angry. She puffed out her chest and ruffled her feathers to show her fury. This was unacceptable! It was her meeting. She was the important one here, not this little human. She paced back and forth, frowning and blinking.

She stormed at them, "My fellow animals, this meeting has been interrupted! I will not have that!"

"I know, I know. This human seems to be more interesting than I am, and you forgot about me and the meeting," continued the owl grumpily. "And it's her fault!" She waved her right wing threateningly at Miya. "This is intolerable. I am holding a meeting!"

Miya felt guilty and ashamed. She hung her head. This was obviously an important meeting for the animals.

"Now waita minute," defended the crow. He gently patted Miya on the back. "She can't help being here—she got lost!" He waved his wings about, yelling.

"She is a human. You know we don't like humans to come here. She trespassed into our forest. This is our place!" replied the squirrel. Outraged, he swished his bushy tail.

The crow turned to face the squirrel. "We can share this forest with the humans. I see them all the time. They don't do anythin' wrong. They like to sit under the trees in the shade when it is hot. I don't see why we can't share."

"SHARE? WITH THOSE HUMANS?! THEY JUST LEAVE GARBAGE AND BREAK THINGS!" CALLED OUT THE SQUIRREL. HE WAS SO ANGRY, HE COULD SPIT!

"HUMANS ARE AWFUL! I KNOW THIS FOR SURE. MY COUSIN TOLD ME. DID YOU KNOW THAT IN THE CITY, THE PEOPLE PUT POISONOUS CHEMICALS ON THE GRASS?" ASKED THE SQUIRREL ANGRILY.

THE LITTLE ANIMALS GASPED IN HORROR.

"AND," CONTINUED THE SQUIRREL, "THEY SPRAY THE TREES WITH POISON AS WELL!"

"OH NO!" CALLED OUT THE CHIPMUNK AND THE FAWN.

"AND THOSE CARS." SAID THE SQUIRREL. "WELL, THEY SMELL. AND THEY KEEP DRIVING EVEN IF OUR COUSINS RUN INTO THE STREET. THEY GET RUN OVER!"

"THAT IS BAD," MUMBLED THE LITTLE BEAR CUB AND THE YOUNG FOX. "REALLY INCONSIDERATE." THEY GLARED AT MIYA.

"I know, I know," the crow shushed his friends. "Not all humans are mean. Look at the people in the village. They give us bread and cookies in the winter. They worry about us. They make sure that we aren't hungry in the winter."

"The factories where they work have chimneys that spit dirty smoke into the air," continued the squirrel, as if he hadn't heard any of the other animals. "My other cousin who lives in the city has breathing problems. It is because of the poisons in the air. The humans call it asthma. My cousin has a human illness."

"Yeah," chimed a small bird. She wiped tears from her little eyes. "A friend of a friend of a friend of mine and her brother got caught in an oil spill. It was so sad. His beautiful white feathers got all stinky and dirty."

"Do you also know that other humans helped the birds get cleaned up again?" asked the crow." See what I mean—the humans aren't all bad."

"But an oil spill should not happen in the first place!" yelled the squirrel from where he sat. "Like I said before, and I'll say it again— humans don't see the consequences of their actions."

"I agree with the squirrel," said the owl gruffly. "The humans are trouble. She is one of them. The owl pointed to Miya. "We don't like her!"

"If you don't watch what you are saying, I'll···I'll···" said the crow. He lifted his fists and waved them around. The smaller animals gasped in surprise. The crow was usually very calm and gentle, and he didn't get angry.

But this topic, about how the humans treated the environment, seemed to get all the animals troubled and upset.

"Oh, please don't argue," said Miya. "I realize that you don't like humans. I know we do things to hurt the environment. But not everyone is like that." She looked over at the squirrel with big eyes. "I'm not like the other humans. I respect nature, and I love animals," said Miya. "Besides, there are lots of humans that think like me."

"Yeah, right," grumbled the squirrel, crossing his arms and turning away.

"Humph," sniffed the owl, puffing out her chest.

"I didn't mean to interrupt your meeting," continued Miya. "I really am lost and just want to go home." She looked at the crow and asked, "Will you show me the way to the edge of the forest?"

"O' course m' girl, o' course," said the crow standing beside her. He gently nudged Miya's shoulder.

"Not until after my meeting!" hooted the owl, as she stomped up and down angrily. "Not until after my meeting!"

The crow shrugged his enormous shoulders. "Whatever!"

He turned to Miya and said, "You can sit. We ain't leavin' yet."

The Animals have a Meeting

Fascinated by her experience of meeting the talking animals, Miya took a seat on an old tree stump next to her new friend, the crow.

"Well," the owl said, fluffing up her brown and black feathers and pushing her chest forward. After all, she was the chairperson, and very important. "As I said before, we won't take this anymore! We won't let the people in the village chase us out of our dens and cut down our homes. They do this all because of a tradition of celebrating the winter solstice" snapped the owl with disgust.

"We don't want those humans to destroy our forest! This is a very serious problem, and we need to find a solution. Who has any ideas? I want to hear some."

"We could chase them away!" shouted the little red fox. He jumped up and down enthusiastically.

"That would be so much fun," squealed a young chipmunk, nodding his little head.

"I know! I know!" yelled the chubby bear cub. "We could make them get lost right here in our own forest. Just like her," he said, pointing to Miya.

"Hooray, hooray," cheered the animals. They thought these were great ideas.

Impatiently, and with a deep frown on her face, the owl paced back and forth. "No! No! None of those ideas will work."

Miya had listened to the animals very quietly. She had never thought about what the animals were saying. She didn't think that she or the villagers had done anything wrong.

THE FOREST WAS PART OF THEIR VILLAGE, AND EVERYONE LOVED IT. THEY LOOKED AFTER IT—TOGETHER. PEOPLE WOULD COME AND HAVE PICNICS AND PLAY IN THE SUMMER. THEY WOULD GO FOR WALKS IN THE SHADE THE FIR TREES PROVIDED IN THE HOT SUMMER MONTHS. IN THE WINTER, THE VILLAGERS OFTEN CAME OUT TO PUT SOME FOOD DOWN SO THE ANIMALS WOULD NOT GO HUNGRY. EVERY YEAR, JUST BEFORE WINTER SOLSTICE, THE PEOPLE WOULD CHOP DOWN THEIR TREES IN THE FOREST. THAT WAS A TRADITION THE VILLAGERS HAD. AFTER ALL, WHAT IS WINTER SOLSTICE WITHOUT A DECORATED TREE?

"MAY I SAY SOMETHING?" WHISPERED MIYA SHYLY.

ENCOURAGINGLY, THE CROW GENTLY PATTED HER ON THE SHOULDER, "SPEAK UP, M' GIRL."

"WELL," SHE BEGAN NERVOUSLY, "WE'VE ALWAYS HAD TREES IN OUR HOMES. BUT WE DIDN'T THINK THAT IT WOULD HURT YOU. HONESTLY, WE REALLY DON'T WANT TO HURT YOU. WE LOVE YOU!"

THE ANIMALS STARED BACK AT HER BLANKLY. SURE ENOUGH, THEY HAD SEEN THIS MANY TIMES. THEY REMEMBERED SEEING THE HUMANS WALK ALONG THE PATHS IN THE FOREST. THEY REMEMBERED WATCHING THE HUMANS SIT AND EAT THEIR FOOD. THEY ESPECIALLY REMEMBERED HOW, EACH YEAR, BRIGHTLY DRESSED BOYS AND GIRLS RAN INTO THE FOREST, WHILE THEIR FATHERS AND MOTHERS SLOWLY FOLLOWED PULLING SLEDS. AND THE ANIMALS REMEMBERED HOW THE HUMANS WOULD EXAMINE ALL THE TREES. THEN THE BOYS AND GIRLS WOULD FIND THE BIGGEST AND STRAIGHTEST ONES TO CHOP DOWN. IT SEEMED THAT THE HUMANS DIDN'T CARE AT ALL IF THE TREES WERE SOMEONE'S HOME, OR THAT CHOPPING THEM DOWN RUINED THE FOREST.

"WE REALLY DIDN'T KNOW WE CHOPPED DOWN YOUR HOMES. HONESTLY!" PLEADED MIYA.

SHE THOUGHT FOR A MOMENT AND SAID, "I THINK… I THINK I COULD HELP YOU FIND A SOLUTION."

Anxiously, she looked at the animals, one by one.

"You!" burst out the owl. "Ha! You are just a small human. What can you do?"

The owl looked very scary and intimidating to Miya. She stepped towards Miya with her feathers fluffed up.

"B...B...But, I think I can help, really I can," stuttered Miya, as she blushed.

"Oh, stop it," replied the owl impatiently, as she paced back and forth.

"Let the girl speak 'er mind", squawked the crow. He protectively put his wing around her shoulders.

For a moment, the owl stood and glared at the crow. Then, with a shrug of her shoulders, she turned her back to the crow, waving her left wing through the air. "If a crow wants to listen to a human girl, it's fine with me, but I won't!" replied the owl angrily.

The crow nodded encouragingly to Miya and patted her on the back. "Go ahead m' girl, go ahead."

Miya began to speak timidly. She noticed how the animals chatted and played with each other. They looked around and paid little attention to her. She noticed that the other animals did not believe she could help. Only the crow seemed interested in what she had to say. But, as Miya spoke, the other animals stopped their fidgeting and fumbling. They leaned forward, so they didn't miss a word of what she said.

"So, I'll go to the village and speak to the people," she finished triumphantly. The animals were so happy with her idea, they jumped up and cheered.

THE CROW GRABBED HER HAND AND SHOOK IT, WHILE THE FAWN AND THE YOUNG BEAR CUB HUGGED EACH OTHER. THE CHIPMUNK JUMPED UP AND DOWN ON A TREE TRUNK, AND THE FOX BEAMED AS IF IT WAS HIS OWN IDEA. SEEING THE OTHER ANIMALS' REACTIONS, THE GRUMPY OWL AND THE GROUCHY SQUIRREL MANAGED TO GRIN TENTATIVELY.

Excited by the wonderful news that Miya was going to talk to the people in the village, the animals set out to show her the way to the edge of the forest. The crow held her hand and walked beside her, very proud of his new human friend.

The fox and the chipmunk skipped ahead of her. The fawn and the chubby bear cub ran ahead of her also, while the owl and the squirrel tagged along behind, shuffling their feet.

They marched steadily on, until the trees came to an abrupt end. There the animals hung back. From this point on, the girl had to go alone. As she started to walk towards the village, the animals waved good-bye.

Miya speaks to the villagers

Snow had fallen, and it had coloured the fields and meadows a peaceful white. A frosty breeze had blown the dark clouds away. Just as Miya reached the top of the snow-covered hill, the sun burst out from behind a cloud.

She stopped to look at the beautiful landscape below. She saw the fields with their corn stubbles peeking out from the snow. She saw how the road continued on into the village. In the distance, she saw the red brick houses with their black shutters and thatched roofs covered with a light scattering of fluffy snow. To the left, she saw the church with its towering steeple. To the right was the village square where some of the people had gathered. For one last moment, she looked at the sight below, and then she slid down the hill towards the village.

Miya strolled along the main street in the direction of the village square. When she arrived, Miya quietly stood and watched as the villagers chatted with each other. She saw her mother standing next to a lamppost talking to one of the other women. Miya waved at her mother, and, with a big warm smile, her mom waved back.

The villagers turned to listen to the mayor who stood in front of all the other villagers. He was a tall man with dark hair and a big moustache. He spoke about the winter solstice and the festivities that would be held in the village.

"We will be decorating the village square the week before the celebrations," began the mayor. "After that we will be ready to bring the children to the forest for our other tradition, the tree-chopping festival. Like last year, we will take the children to the forest a week before the winter solstice celebrations to chop our trees. That way, the trees will be fresh for the celebration," boomed the mayor. His moustache bounced up and down as he spoke.

"Are we going to have the tree-burning ceremony this year?" asked someone in the crowd.

"Well," said the mayor as he scratched his head. "Yes! We can probably do that a week after the celebrations."

Miya listened, appalled by what the mayor was saying. Cutting down trees, and then, after the celebrations, burning them. "My goodness," she thought. "How could we do such things to the environment?" She had never thought about it before, but it was really not a very friendly thing to do to nature.

Her mind raced as she thought about what she had told the animals. She tried to find something to say to the villagers. She wanted to make them understand that they shouldn't cut down the trees. Not this year, or next year, or the year after that. What she heard about burning the trees was awful! They needed a new tradition. She needed to do something to convince the villagers to save the trees and help her new animal friends.

"Could you maybe··· well···" stuttered Miya. She stopped, embarrassed. "Maybe··· well··· Don't chop down the trees! It is horrible!" she blurted out with tears in her eyes. Shocked by her own courage, she stopped short and felt a deep blush creep up into her face.

The mayor turned to look at her. "What?!" he burst out. "Not chop down the trees! What do you mean?"

"I···I···" tried Miya. She hung her head. Intimidated by the mayor and his big moustache, she turned to walk away. But then she remembered her new animal friends. She thought of the crow, the fox, the fawn, the chubby bear cub, the chipmunk, and even the owl and the squirrel. They were all depending on her to help save their forest. She straightened her back, and, knowing she was doing the right thing, she turned around.

With determination in her voice, Miya said loudly, "It is wrong to chop down trees in the forest. The animals live there. The trees are their homes, and they don't want to lose their homes!"

"What's wrong with chopping down some trees?" yelled the mayor as he pursed his lips, pushing out his moustache.

The crowd murmured in agreement, "Really! There is nothing wrong with chopping down trees!"

Miya stood in front of the villagers. With tears in her eyes, she looked into the crowd, forlorn. All she could see were blank faces staring back at her. She felt alone and looked around for a friendly face. Then she saw her mother who gave her a big smile and nodded encouragingly.
This gave Miya the courage to continue. She smiled back at her mother. With her support, Miya started to explain to the villagers how the animals felt about the actions of the humans.

Miya sniffed, wiped her tears away, and started to talk. She talked and talked. She talked about the owl who had called a meeting, because she was so concerned about her forest. She talked about the grumpy squirrel who was so suspicious of humans. She talked about the crow who believed in the goodness of the humans and defended them. Miya described how the fox was always happy to play tricks and laugh, and how the chubby bear cub loved to roll around on his back and play with the other little animals. She told the villagers about the timid fawn and the cute chipmunk who would frolic and tease the squirrel. Most importantly, she described to the villagers how the animals loved their forest and wanted to save their homes. Miya stood tall and felt wonderful as she worked to help the animals.

"Well, that is very sweet, little girl, but what do you want us to do about it?" challenged a woman. "After all, what is a winter solstice celebration without a decorated tree in our home? That is our tradition."

"OKAY, I'VE GOT AN IDEA. WE CAN CREATE A NEW TRADITION," SAID MIYA.
"LISTEN CAREFULLY. I THINK YOU WILL LIKE IT."

ONCE SHE SPOKE WITH THE VILLAGERS, SHE WAVED GOOD-BYE TO THEM.
SHE CALLED TO HER MOTHER, "I'VE GOT TO TELL THE ANIMALS. I'LL BE
HOME SOON."

BEFORE HER MOTHER COULD SAY ANYTHING, MIYA RAN OFF IN THE DIRECTION
OF THE FOREST.

Miya happily ran along the road and up the hill. Her cheeks were a brilliant red, and her eyes shone brightly. Dusk had fallen by the time Miya started to make her way to the forest. The wind had calmed down, and snow had stopped falling. The clouds had drifted away, and a few stars were already twinkling in the darkening sky.

Miya was very eager to tell her animal friends the good news. It wouldn't be long now. After listening to her, the people in the village had promised not to chop down any of the trees. They wanted to be friends with the animals, just like she did.

Miya saw her new friends from a distance, hugging the outskirts of the forest. Eagerly, they had waited for her to return. As Miya got closer, she waved at them and shouted enthusiastically, "They won't chop down the trees! They won't chop down the trees!"

A Day of celebrations

It had been a few days since Miya had visited, and the animals began to relax. Fresh snow gently fell, and a cold mist hung under the trees. The forest was calm and quiet. The villagers had not come to the forest to chop down any trees, just as they had promised.

It was the morning of the winter solstice celebration, and the forest was alive with the hustle and bustle of the animals. The animals were excited as they busily gathered food, played, and visited each other. The preparations for their own winter celebrations were underway.

The crow, who was the master of ceremonies, called out to the other animals to come gather together in their meeting place. It was almost time for their very own special ceremony. One by one the animals arrived.

The chipmunk sat on the old hollow tree trunk and the squirrel perched on a stump. A few of the little birds rested in the old, gnarly oak tree, while the fox and the fawn settled under the tree. The chubby bear cub plopped onto the frozen ground and propped his front paws under his chin.

"Tank yo' fer comin' together. It's almos' time te prepare fer de ceremony!" said the crow. "Who has somethin' te say about the pas' year?"

"I do!" replied the owl. "We have been very lucky this year. We had a peaceful and happy year, and nothing really bad happened in our forest."

THE OTHER ANIMALS NODDED IN AGREEMENT. THEY ALL KNEW ABOUT THEIR COUSINS WHO LIVED IN THE OTHER FORESTS. IT HAD BEEN A DIFFICULT YEAR FOR THEM. THERE WERE FIRES IN SOME FORESTS, AND IN OTHER FORESTS THERE HAD BEEN NO RAIN, SO THEY WERE VERY DRY AND FOOD WAS SCARCE.

"WELL," CONTINUED THE CROW, "WE NEED TE BE T'ANKFUL AN' PROMISE TE LOOK AFTER OUR FOREST AN' EACH OTHER FER DE NEX' YEAR. NOW COME STAND WIT' ME."

THE CLOUDS IN THE SKY HAD FLOATED AWAY, AND, WHILE THE SUN HAD SET, DUSK HAD SETTLED OVER THE FOREST. QUIETLY, ALL THE ANIMALS GOT UP AND STOOD IN A CIRCLE. THEY CLASPED PAWS AND WINGS TOGETHER, AND, THROUGH THE TREETOPS, THEY PEERED UP TO THE SKY, WAITING. A FEW SOFT SNOWFLAKES FLOATED DOWN FROM THE BRANCHES AND LANDED ON THEIR EAGER, UPTURNED FACES.

"Oh," gasped the bear cub. "Look, Look, I see it. I see the first star! It's the Northern Star."

The other animals held their breath and nodded. This was an emotional and moving moment. This was the beginning of their festival, the winter solstice celebration.

Calmly, the owl took a deep breath. The other animals stirred and looked at each other. It was time. Then, while all the animals looked up to the star again, the owl quietly mumbled, "We, the dwellers of the forest, pledge to look after the earth, the forest, and each other. This we promise."

"This we promise," murmured the chubby bear cub and the fox. "This we promise," said the squirrel and the fawn. "This we promise," whispered the crow and the owl. "This we promise," chirped the little birds.

For a few minutes all the animals gazed up at the star. Then the crow called out, "Tis time te have fun an' eat!"

All the animals had brought some of their gatherings and had put them in a pile near the old, gnarly oak tree. This was their yearly feast. There were berries, nuts, and seeds to share. There was some honey that the bear cub had saved especially for this celebration. There were pine cones and pieces of juicy bark. There were even a few pieces of old bread and dried biscuits that some of the animals had saved from the times the villagers had spread them out for the animals.

The owl had worked very hard. She had prepared a special drink from water saved from the rain in a bucket made from the bark of the fir trees. In the bucket the owl had put a few berries and some honey and a few pine needles. Then all the ingredients had to soak for a week. It tasted sweet and all the animals loved it.

A FEW OF THE LITTLE BIRDS WERE SINGING AND THE FAWN AND CHIPMUNK WERE DANCING. THE SQUIRREL WAS SURROUNDED BY OTHER ANIMALS, WHILE HE TOLD THE STORIES OF THE HUMANS IN THE CITY.

THE FOX WAS TEASING THE BEAR CUB WHO WAS LICKING HIS PAWS WHICH WERE STICKY WITH HONEY.

ALL THE ANIMALS WERE EATING, DANCING, AND DRINKING WHEN A FEW GOSSIPY SPARROWS CAME TO GIVE THEN SOME STARTLING NEWS.

"WE SAW A FEW ADULTS AND CHILDREN WALKING THROUGH THE CORNFIELDS TOWARDS THE FOREST," CHIRPED THE SPARROWS. "YES, THE HUMANS ARE DEFIANTLY COMING TO THE FOREST."

THE FOX AND THE BEAR CUB GASPED IN SURPRISE. THE CHIPMUNK STOPPED DANCING AND NERVOUSLY PACED UP AND DOWN THE FALLEN TREE TRUNK. THE FAWN GIGGLED ANXIOUSLY, AND THE SQUIRREL AND THE OWL HAD DEEP FROWNS ON THEIR FACES. THEY WERE VERY WORRIED.

"DO YOU KNOW WHY THESE HUMANS ARE ON THEIR WAY?" ASKED THE SQUIRREL.

"NO, WE DON'T," TWITTERED ONE OF THE SPARROWS. "WE DID NOTICE THAT THEY HAVE LARGE BAGS WITH THEM."

"Do they have axes and saws with them?" asked the owl, her voice trembling with anxiety.

"We couldn't see any," replied the sparrows. "We circled around a few times, but we couldn't tell if they had axes or saws."

"Are the villagers coming to chop down the trees anyway?" asked the fox. This was very alarming.

"The people promised us they would not chop down the trees. Isn't that what Miya told us?" asked the bear cub.

"Maybe the villagers are going to break their promise. You know how humans are!" sniffed the squirrel.

"Does anyone know what Miya told the villagers?" asked the crow.

"No, we forgot to ask her," wailed the fawn, "We were so excited about the news, we forgot to ask Miya what she had said!"

The animals didn't know what to expect, and this made them very, very nervous.

There was a tension in the air. The fir trees stood perfectly still, as if they too were nervously waiting for what was to come.

The celebrations had suddenly stopped, and the animals huddled in their dens, alone with their thoughts. They waited and waited. What if the humans came to cut down the trees? What if they didn't keep their promise?

It got later and later, and, when they could not stay awake any longer, the animals fell asleep, one by one.

A BIG SURPRISE

WINTER SOLSTICE MORNING WAS QUIET, AND EVERYTHING LOOKED PEACEFUL, CALM, AND UNDISTURBED. THE TREES SWAYED SLIGHTLY, AS A SOFT BREEZE PLAYED LIGHTLY THROUGH THE TREETOPS. AS THE EARLY DAYLIGHT BEGAN TO BRIGHTEN THE SKY, THE ANIMALS STIRRED.

THE CROW SLEEPILY BALANCED ON A BRANCH. YAWNING, HE CALMLY STRETCHED HIS WINGS. HE RUBBED HIS EYES, OPENING THEM ONE AT A TIME. HE TOOK A DEEP BREATH AND LOOKED AROUND TO SEE IF ANYONE ELSE WAS AWAKE. HE GASPED WITH DELIGHT! WHAT HE SAW WAS BEAUTIFUL!

"WOW! GUYS, COME ON OUT 'N' SEE THIS! WOW!" HE SQUAWKED. "YOU'VE GOT TE SEE THIS!" JUMPING UP AND DOWN WITH EXCITEMENT, THE CROW SHOUTED LOUDLY.

THE YOUNG FOX AND THE CHIPMUNK GROGGILY CAME OUT OF THEIR DENS AND LOOKED AROUND. RUBBING THEIR EYES SLEEPILY, THE BEAR CUB AND THE FAWN POKED THEIR HEADS OUT. WHAT THEY SAW WAS UNBELIEVABLE.

THRILLED BY WHAT THEY SAW, THE ANIMALS ALL DANCED AROUND IN A CIRCLE. THEY SHOUTED OUT IN EXCITEMENT. THE OWL AND THE SQUIRREL CAME OUT OF THEIR HOMES TO SEE WHAT THE FUSS WAS ALL ABOUT.

"WHAT IS ALL THE NOISE ABOUT? I WANT TO SLEEP!" GRUMBLED THE SQUIRREL.

"THIS IS SO UNDIGNIFIED!" SNIFFED THE OWL.

"BUT LOOK," CALLED THE CROW." LOOK'T ALL THIS." JUMPING UP AND DOWN, HE POINTED IN ALL DIRECTIONS.

Astonished by what they saw, they stood side by side and stared…

All around them, the animals saw beautiful ribbons. Red ones, blue ones, green ones, and white ones were draped from tree to tree. Twinkling lights were strung from branch to branch. Brightly coloured glass trinkets of all shapes and sizes were hung from almost every branch and bush. A faint clinking sound could be heard as the wind brushed the trinkets against each other.

The animals were overjoyed by the spectacular sight, their eyes sparkling with delight. The people from the village had given them a big, big surprise.

"See, the humans ain't all tha' bad!" The crow had always believed that humans were not so terrible.

"Humph," the owl and the squirrel admitted begrudgingly. "Okay, maybe not all the humans are bad. Miya is a good human after all."

THE ANIMALS DANCED AND DANCED. THEY ARRIVED AT THE EDGE OF THE FOREST, AND THE CROW REALIZED THAT SOME OF THE VILLAGERS WERE STANDING IN THE CORNFIELD. THEY WERE WATCHING WITH SMILES ON THEIR FACES. THEY WATCHED HOW THEIR NEW ANIMAL FRIENDS WERE OVERJOYED WITH THEIR SURPRISE. THEY WATCHED HOW THE FAWN DANCED LIGHTLY THROUGH THE SNOW, AND HOW THE BEAR CUB AND THE CHIPMUNK HUGGED EACH OTHER, AND HOW THE FOX RACED AROUND THE TREES. THEY SAW THAT ALL THE OTHER LITTLE ANIMALS HAD COME OUT TO SEE WHAT WAS HAPPENING.

THE CROW STOPPED FOR A MOMENT, BECAUSE HE REALIZED THE HUMANS WERE WAITING. WHEN THE OTHER ANIMALS NOTICED THAT THE CROW HAD STOPPED DANCING, THEY STOPPED TO SEE WHAT THE CROW WAS STARING AT. THE ANIMALS SAW THE HUMANS STANDING IN THE CORNFIELD AND FROZE. THIS WAS STRANGE, AND A BIT SCARY, SO MANY HUMANS.

THEN THE CROW SAW HIS NEW FRIEND, MIYA, AND HELD OUT HIS LEFT WING. SHE GRABBED IT, SO HE COULD TWIRL HER AROUND IN A CIRCLE. WHEN THE OTHER ANIMALS SAW THIS, THEY ALL REACHED OUT TO THE HUMANS. ONE BY ONE, THEY GRABBED THE VILLAGERS' HANDS. PAW IN HAND, THE ANIMALS AND THE HUMANS DANCED INTO THE FOREST.

MIYA WATCHED HER MOTHER DANCE WITH THE FAWN. THE MAYOR DANCED WITH THE CHUBBY BEAR CUB. THE SAME WOMAN WHO CHALLENGED MIYA AT THE MEETING IN THE VILLAGE SQUARE WALTZED WITH THE FOX. THE CHIPMUNK WAS TWIRLING AND TWIRLING UNTIL HE GOT DIZZY.

THE ANIMALS FELT A WARM GLOW IN THEIR HEARTS AS THEY SHARED THEIR WINTER CELEBRATION WITH THE HUMANS. THE VILLAGERS HAD SHOWN THE ANIMALS THAT THEY DID CARE AND WANTED TO SHARE THEIR WINTER SOLSTICE CELEBRATIONS WITH THEM.

THE OWL AND THE SQUIRREL STOOD TO ONE SIDE AND WATCHED ALL THE EXCITEMENT. THEY BOTH HAD SILLY GRINS ON THEIR FACES. IT WAS A GREAT DAY, AND THEY SAW THAT THE HUMANS WERE NOT ALL BAD, JUST AS MIYA HAD TOLD THEM. THEY WALKED TOWARDS THE CROW AND MIYA. THEY JOINED IN, AND THE FOUR OF THEM DANCED AND TWIRLED AROUND AND AROUND.

Quietly, the squirrel took Miya aside and gave her a big hug.

He had tears in his eyes as he whispered, "This is the best winter solstice celebration we've ever had! And a wonderful new tradition for all of us." said the squirrel with a happy smile on his face.

"Thank you, Miya. Thank you for saving our forest."

The End

DiDi LeMay enjoys a busy life writing, teaching English as a Second Language, and helping her students find their career paths.

She was involved with children's entertainment for numerous years. While living in Europe she founded a Children's Theatre Group, teaching children the ins and outs of acting, dancing, stage management, and writing. Eventually, teaching and writing took up most of her time.

DiDi's hobbies are reading and learning about the environment, as well as nutrition and good health.

DiDi is happily married and lives in Toronto, Canada with her husband and two cats.

Printed in the United States
125704LV00003B